E
Freeman,
Tor
c.3

For my dad,

John Freeman,

who knows how

to keep a secret

Copyright © 2012 by Tor Freeman

Produced by Brubaker, Ford & Friends

First U.S. edition 2012

Library of Congress Cataloging-in-Publication Data is available.
Library of Congress Catalog Card Number pending
ISBN 978-0-7636-6149-6

12 13 14 15 16 17 TLF 10 9 8 7 6 5 4 3 2 1

Printed in Dongguan, Guangdong, China

This book was typeset in Stempel Schneidler.
The illustrations were done in mixed media.

TEMPLAR BOOKS

an imprint of Candlewick Press
99 Dover Street
Somerville, Massachusetts 02144

www.candlewick.com

OLIVE
AND THE BIG
SECRET

TOR FREEMAN

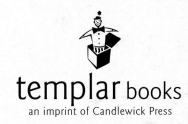

templar books
an imprint of Candlewick Press

Molly told Olive  a secret.

"You mustn't tell anyone," said Molly.

"I will never tell," said Olive.

So now Olive had a secret.

Olive knew she should
keep the secret to herself.
She knew she shouldn't
tell anyone.
But . . .

maybe she
would just
tell her
friend Jessie.

But really,
she shouldn't.

Olive couldn't stop
thinking about the secret.
She thought about it
while she jumped rope.
She knew she shouldn't tell.
But . . .

Olive thought
she would just
tell her friend
Ziggy.

"Guess what!"
Olive said. "What?"
said Ziggy.

"Oh . . .
nothing,"
said Olive.

This secret was
really hard to keep!
Olive thought she would
just tell her friend Joe.

So she did.

"But you can't
tell anyone,"
said Olive.

Now
Joe had
a secret.

He thought about it
all the way to his
swimming lesson.

He thought about it in the locker room.

He knew he shouldn't tell, but . . .

Joe thought
he'd just tell his
friend Matt.

Splutter!
said Matt.

"But you can't tell
anyone," said Joe.

Now Matt had a secret.
Matt wasn't very good
at keeping secrets.

He told the first
friends he saw —
Lola and Bea.

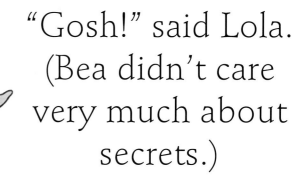

"Gosh!" said Lola.
(Bea didn't care
very much about
secrets.)

Now Lola had a secret.
She thought about
it while she finished
her milk shake.

Then she said
good-bye
to Bea.

She
couldn't
wait to tell,
because . . .

Lola's best friend was Molly,
and Lola told her
everything!

Molly's secret was out.

And she knew just
who had told it.

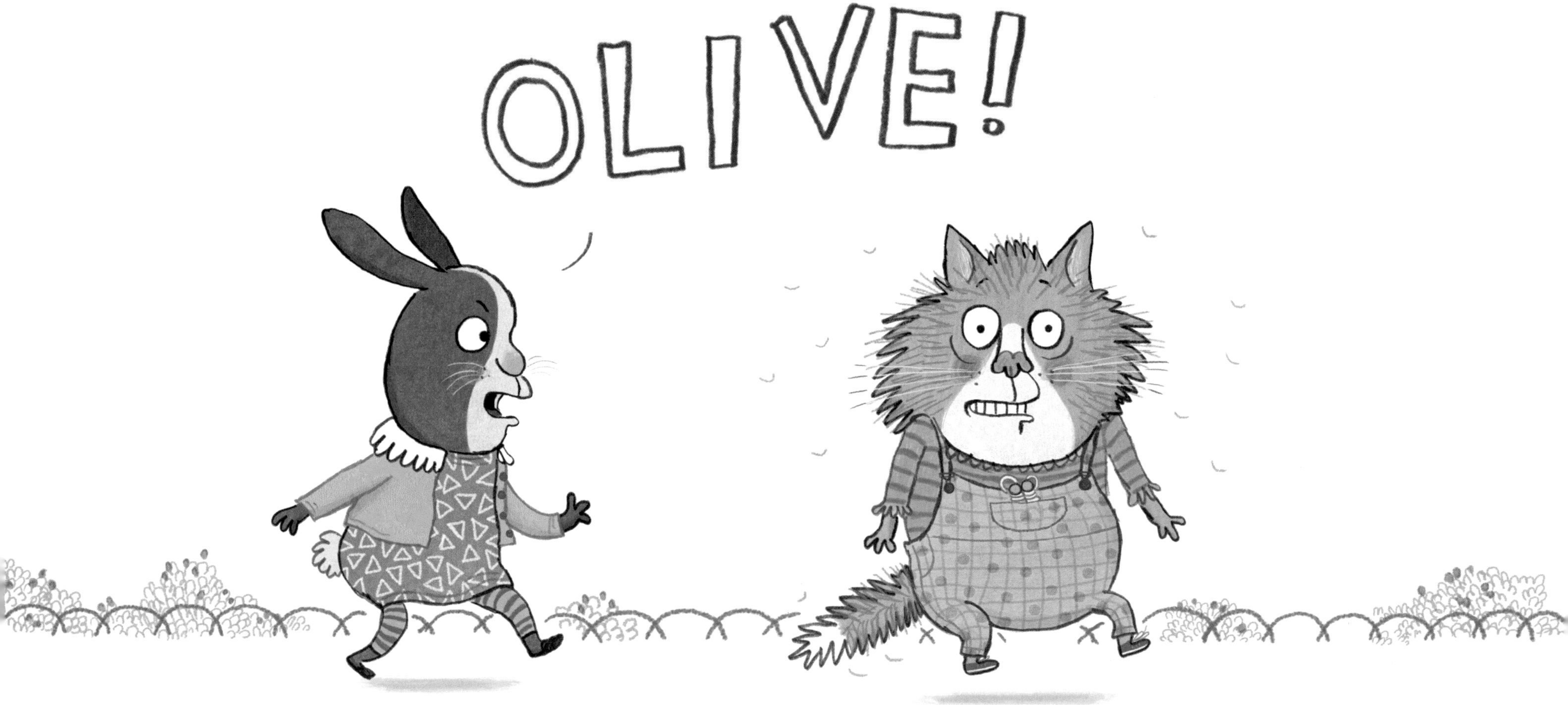
OLIVE!

And
do
you
want
to
know

what
Molly

told
Olive,

who
told Joe,

who
told Matt,

who
told Lola,

who told
Molly?

Well,
I'd like
to tell
you,

but . . .

IT'S A SECRET!

Pssst—